MobLand

A Deep Dive Into Family, Power, and Crime in Modern TV Drama

By kingsley Freeman

"MobLand: A Deep Dive Into Family, Power, and Crime in Modern TV Drama"

Dive deep into the world of MobLand, the gripping crime drama that has captivated audiences worldwide. This in-depth exploration offers a comprehensive look at the series, examining its complex characters, intricate plotlines, and the remarkable performances from stars like Tom Hardy, Pierce Brosnan, and Helen Mirren.

From the show's inception and development under the visionary direction of Guy Ritchie, to its behind-the-scenes challenges, this book uncovers everything you need to know about the making of MobLand. Get exclusive insights into the creative process, from scriptwriting to location scouting, and discover how the show's production team overcame obstacles to create a unique and immersive crime world.

Uncover the lasting impact MobLand has had on the crime drama genre, delving into its themes of family, loyalty, power, and morality. The book also touches on the show's cultural influence, fan reactions, and the potential future of the series, including speculation about new characters, plotlines, and possible spin-offs.

Whether you're a MobLand fan or a lover of TV drama, this book is your ultimate guide to understanding the world behind one of the most exciting crime series in recent years.

Table of contents

Introduction

Overview of "MobLand" as a Cultural Phenomenon

When it comes to crime dramas, few have captured the attention of audiences with the same fervor as MobLand. Premiering in late March 2025, this gripping crime series quickly became a topic of conversation not only for its high-stakes storytelling but also for its star-studded cast, led by the renowned Guy Ritchie. With its intense exploration of crime, power, and family dynamics, MobLand taps into a cultural fascination with organized crime that has existed for decades in popular media.

The show's plot, which centers around two rival crime families, draws on a well-established tradition of gangster tales, yet it offers a fresh perspective that reflects modern societal issues and complex characters. Through the lens of the Harrigan and Stevenson families, MobLand reflects themes of loyalty, betrayal, ambition, and the brutal consequences of life within a criminal empire. These stories resonate with viewers, drawing on the appeal of power struggles, intergenerational conflicts, and moral ambiguity. In many ways, the show has come to embody a new era of crime dramas, where the line between hero and villain is increasingly difficult to discern.

While MobLand takes cues from its predecessors in the genre, it introduces new layers to the storytelling, particularly through its focus on character depth and personal stakes. For its audience, the show is not just about the crime; it is about the people who are caught up in it, and how their choices—driven by desperation, love, or ambition—shape the outcome of their lives. As MobLand continues to unfold, it becomes clear that the show is not merely a continuation of a well-worn genre, but a redefinition of it, making it a significant cultural moment in the world of television.

Brief Summary of the Crime Drama Series' Release and Significance

The series debuted on Paramount+ in March 2025, with the premiere episode marking the beginning of what is expected to be a gripping and suspense-filled journey. MobLand immediately stood out due to its impressive production values and the involvement of some of Hollywood's biggest names. Starring Tom Hardy, Pierce Brosnan, and Helen Mirren, the show has been able to attract both critical acclaim and a dedicated fanbase, thanks to the star power and compelling performances of its cast.

What sets MobLand apart from other crime dramas is its ability to blend traditional gangster tropes with modern sensibilities. The world of organized crime is often portrayed in stark, violent terms, but MobLand chooses to explore the psychological and emotional turmoil of its characters, offering viewers not just the thrill of crime but the human cost behind it. The series also touches on broader societal issues such as class, loyalty, and the impact of legacy, all while maintaining a fast-paced and engaging plot.

In a television landscape crowded with crime dramas, MobLand managed to carve out a distinct identity, sparking conversations about its relevance and influence. Its release was met with a mix of anticipation and skepticism—questions surrounding whether it could live up to the hype generated by its promotional campaign. Yet, as episodes unfolded, the show's deepening narrative, strong character development, and complex moral dilemmas quickly quelled any doubts, establishing MobLand as a series to watch in the years to come.

The show's success also comes at a time when crime dramas are experiencing a resurgence, partly due to the ongoing fascination with stories of organized crime and the criminal underworld. This cultural moment, coupled with MobLand's ability to tap into the zeitgeist, has ensured its place as a noteworthy addition to the genre.

Objective and Approach of the Book

This book aims to provide a comprehensive, objective, and nuanced exploration of MobLand as both a television series and a cultural touchstone. It will dive deep into the key aspects of the show that have contributed to its success, examining everything from the creative forces behind it to the performances of its cast and its reception by both critics and audiences.

In crafting this book, the goal is not to offer a biased perspective but to present a balanced view of the series' significance. By focusing on the facts, research, and analysis, the book will allow readers to gain a deeper understanding of why MobLand has resonated so strongly with viewers. It will explore the technical aspects of production, the thematic elements that run through the storylines, and the way in which the series interacts with larger societal issues.

As a neutral account, the book will provide an informative look at the impact of MobLand on the crime drama genre, while also acknowledging its limitations and areas where it may not appeal to every viewer. The approach will be journalistic, focused on uncovering the facts, presenting them clearly, and offering insights into what makes the show a standout within its category.

Through this analysis, the book will offer a comprehensive overview of MobLand, illuminating the various layers that have helped make it a significant cultural and entertainment phenomenon. It will serve as both an in-depth examination for those who are already fans of the show and a valuable resource for those unfamiliar with the series but curious about its broader cultural implications.

Chapter 1: Origins of "MobLand"

History of the Series Concept

The concept of MobLand emerged at a time when crime dramas were experiencing a resurgence in global popularity. However, the series does not simply adhere to the traditional formula of gritty street-level crime. It sought to address something deeper—exploring the psychological and emotional intricacies of the criminal world, the complex relationships within organized crime families, and the price of loyalty and power. In this, MobLand differentiates itself from previous crime dramas by focusing not only on the criminal activity but on the personal lives and moral dilemmas of its characters.

The idea for MobLand reportedly originated from a long-standing desire within the television industry to bring a modern yet timeless exploration of family dynasties and organized crime to the screen. Crime families have been a consistent theme in cinema and television for decades, with shows like The Sopranos, Breaking Bad, and films such as The Godfather offering iconic takes on the genre. MobLand was conceived with the intention of updating this narrative by introducing complex characters within a more contemporary context, while retaining the age-old themes of betrayal, ambition, and vengeance.

Although its premise might seem familiar—feuding crime families, family loyalty, violent retribution—the show's creative vision aimed to refresh the genre with a modern sensibility. Its emphasis on nuanced character development, rather than relying solely on crime scenes and action, marked it as a unique offering. By placing a greater focus on the human side of the story—on both the victims and perpetrators—MobLand sought to invite audiences into the emotional and moral conflicts faced by its characters.

Development Timeline and How the Idea Came to Fruition

The development of MobLand began in the early months of 2023, when initial discussions were held between key figures in the entertainment industry. At the time, the success of gritty crime thrillers and gangster films, particularly those in the vein of Guy Ritchie's earlier work, had proven the genre's continued appeal to a global audience. However, there was a sense that many crime stories had become formulaic. With a fresh creative approach in mind, the development team set out to craft a narrative that would resonate with viewers both familiar and new to the genre.

During these early stages, the creators recognized the growing demand for streaming content that could provide long-form storytelling over multiple seasons. Paramount+, the platform that would eventually house the series, was keen on tapping into this demand for high-quality crime drama that could also generate significant buzz. It wasn't long before a development team was assembled to shape the show's tone, aesthetic, and narrative direction.

By the middle of 2023, Guy Ritchie, known for his distinctive take on crime stories in films like Lock, Stock and Two Smoking Barrels and Snatch, was brought on board as the show's director and executive producer. Ritchie's involvement was crucial in cementing the project's identity. His signature style—character-driven storytelling laced with wit, dark humor, and sharp dialogue—seemed to be the perfect fit for a series centered around morally complex gangsters. While Ritchie's films had traditionally focused on the underworld of London, MobLand would mark his first major venture into serialized television, allowing for a deeper exploration of characters over time.

With Ritchie on board, the development accelerated. Writers and producers worked quickly to finalize the show's vision, ensuring that the characters would not only be deeply flawed but also deeply relatable. The aim was to humanize the criminals—making their actions both understandable and tragic—while also depicting the high stakes that come with life in the underworld.

Background on Guy Ritchie's Involvement and His Vision

Guy Ritchie's name is synonymous with modern British crime storytelling. His films have often centered on the chaotic and sometimes absurd dynamics of street-level crime, capturing the grit of the criminal world while balancing moments of sharp humor and brilliant character interplay. With MobLand, Ritchie was drawn to the opportunity to develop a television series that would expand the scale of his crime storytelling, allowing for more complex narratives and deeper character exploration.

For Ritchie, the prospect of tackling the idea of family within a crime context was especially appealing. The criminal underworld has long been depicted as a series of power struggles, alliances, and betrayals, but Ritchie sought to delve into the emotional intricacies of family ties in a high-stakes environment. Through MobLand, he hoped to highlight the sacrifices that family members make, not just in terms of loyalty to their criminal organizations, but also to each other. This vision became the backbone of the show's central conflict, with the Harrigan and Stevenson families embodying the push and pull between ambition and kinship.

Ritchie's experience as a director also helped to shape the show's visual style. Known for his fast-paced editing, sharp dialogue, and compelling action sequences, he brought a cinematic flair to the series. Yet, he was equally focused on capturing quieter, more intimate moments that showcased the psychological depth of the characters. Ritchie's signature style would not only define the show's aesthetic but also its pacing, which moves quickly while still leaving room for reflection and character development.

One of Ritchie's key objectives was to create a series that could stand out within the crowded landscape of crime dramas. While many shows in the genre have centered on mafia families or street-level gangs, Ritchie's vision for MobLand was to make it both a character study and a high-stakes thriller. His understanding of how crime affects people on a deeply personal level allowed him to inject MobLand with a sense of realism, ensuring that even the most extreme actions in the series were grounded in human motivations.

The Initial Announcement and Casting Decisions

The initial announcement of MobLand was met with much anticipation, especially when it was revealed that Guy Ritchie would be at the helm. His involvement was a major draw for fans of his previous work, and the news immediately stirred interest in both the entertainment and television industries. The project was officially unveiled to the public in late 2023, with Paramount+ confirming that the series world premiere in March 2025.

The casting of MobLand played a crucial role in generating buzz for the show. Tom Hardy was the first major star to be attached to the project, playing the role of Harry Da Souza, a fixer working for the Harrigan family. Hardy, known for his intense performances and versatile acting range, was seen as the perfect fit for a role that demanded both physicality and emotional depth. His character, a man caught between his loyalties to his family and his personal struggles, was always meant to be the moral center of the series.

Shortly after Hardy's casting, Pierce Brosnan and Helen Mirren joined the project, playing the patriarch and matriarch of the Harrigan crime family. Brosnan, known for his suave and commanding screen presence, was cast as Conrad Harrigan, the aging yet ruthless leader of the family. Mirren, a veteran of both dramatic and action roles, was brought in to portray Maeve Harrigan, a strong-willed matriarch with her own complex moral compass.

The casting decisions were critical in shaping the overall tone of MobLand. Ritchie's choice of established, high-caliber actors allowed the show to maintain its focus on character-driven storytelling while ensuring a strong sense of credibility. The decision to cast Hardy, Brosnan, and Mirren in key roles indicated that MobLand would not merely be another run-of-the-mill crime drama but rather a layered exploration of its characters' lives, relationships, and choices.

The announcement of the show's core cast generated considerable excitement within the industry. Fans were eager to see how Hardy, in particular, would tackle a role in a crime drama, after his previous work in films such as The Dark Knight Rises and Mad Max: Fury Road. Similarly, Brosnan's portrayal of a crime boss and Mirren's as a powerful matriarch suggested a compelling dynamic at the heart of the series, one that promised to be both thrilling and emotionally resonant.

Together, these elements—the strong concept, Ritchie's creative vision, and the high-profile cast—formed the foundation upon which MobLand would be built. As development progressed into 2024, the series began to take shape, promising an exciting and nuanced portrayal of crime, family, and loyalty that would captivate audiences when it finally premiered.

Chapter 2: The Plot and Storyline

In-depth Analysis of the Plot

MobLand unravels as an intricate exploration of organized crime, power dynamics, and familial ties within two competing crime families, the Harrigans and the Stevensons. Set in a sprawling, fictional urban landscape where the lines between law and lawlessness are blurred, the plot delves into the unyielding loyalty, betrayal, and ambition that drive the lives of its central characters.

At its core, MobLand revolves around Harry Da Souza (played by Tom Hardy), a highly skilled "fixer" working for the Harrigan family. The story kicks off when Eddie Harrigan, the reckless grandson of Conrad and Maeve Harrigan (played by Pierce Brosnan and Helen Mirren), makes a dangerous misstep that sets off a chain of events threatening both his family and their criminal empire. This seemingly minor error snowballs into a high-stakes conflict with the rival Stevenson family, led by patriarch Richard Stevenson, a man with his own power-hungry ambitions.

The central narrative arc is propelled by the escalating tension between the two families, with Harry caught in the middle. His role as a fixer makes him integral to the survival of the Harrigan clan, yet as the conflict intensifies, Harry's personal code of morality is tested.

His relationships with the Harrigan family, particularly with Conrad and Maeve, grow increasingly complicated as their goals become more at odds. As the series progresses, Harry's loyalties are stretched to the limit, culminating in decisions that will have profound consequences not only for him but for the entire crime organization he serves.

The plot is heavily character-driven, and as it unfolds, viewers are introduced to several secondary characters—each of whom plays a crucial role in the ongoing drama. One of the most compelling elements of the show is the tension between Harry and other key figures within the Harrigan family, particularly Maeve, whose ruthless leadership style is sometimes at odds with Harry's more empathetic approach. This dynamic provides both a source of conflict and an exploration of what it means to serve a family that has such morally complex leaders.

Throughout the season, key events continuously challenge the stability of the Harrigan family empire. The fateful encounter between Eddie and the Stevensons not only forces the two families to confront one another directly but also reveals the deeper issues within the Harrigan family itself, including generational divides, old debts, and the blurred line between personal and professional allegiances.

The narrative's forward momentum is driven by power struggles, shifting alliances, and the personal stakes of each character. As new players are introduced and old scores are settled, the stakes continue to rise. The tension between Harry's desire for a better life and the weight of his obligations to the Harrigan family serves as one of the series' most intriguing undercurrents.

Key Events and the Central Conflict

The inciting incident of MobLand occurs in the early episodes, when Eddie Harrigan, in an attempt to assert his own power within the family, makes an ill-advised move against a member of the rival Stevenson family. This action sets off a series of retaliatory strikes, which escalates into full-scale hostilities between the two clans. Eddie's reckless ambition, combined with his lack of respect for the family legacy, introduces the central conflict that drives the series forward.

As the hostilities between the two families grow more intense, the show delves into the devastating effects that these external conflicts have on the internal dynamics of the Harrigan family. Conrad Harrigan, the family patriarch, faces mounting pressure to protect his legacy and his empire. His cold, calculating nature comes to the forefront as he grapples with the idea of preserving his family's power at any cost.

Maeve Harrigan, his wife, is equally focused on the survival of the family business, but her leadership style is defined by her ability to manipulate the emotions of those around her. A central event in the first season involves Maeve's decision to leverage a long-standing family secret to her advantage, further deepening the rift between her and Conrad, while also introducing Harry Da Souza as a figure who may serve as a bridge—or a threat—to the fractured family.

The central conflict, therefore, is twofold: the direct animosity between the Harrigans and the Stevensons, and the internal disarray caused by familial strife. Harry's loyalty to the family is continually tested by the tension between what he believes is right and the demands of his role within the clan. His growing desire to carve out a life separate from the Harrigans becomes increasingly difficult as the plot progresses, creating a compelling tension between his personal and professional worlds.

As the conflict intensifies, a turning point arrives when Conrad is forced to make a difficult decision regarding the future of the family's criminal operations. This decision, which involves an alliance with an external figure, introduces new power players and raises the stakes even higher. Meanwhile, the Stevensons, who are led by the ruthless Richard Stevenson, begin to counterattack with their own strategic moves, bringing further chaos to an already volatile situation.

Overview of Major Story Arcs

The overarching story arc of MobLand involves the rise and fall of the Harrigan family, as seen through the eyes of Harry Da Souza. However, several subplots run parallel to the central narrative, each contributing to the development of the characters and the broader world of the show.

1. Harry Da Souza's Moral Dilemma: One of the most prominent subplots revolves around Harry's struggle with his role in the criminal underworld. A man who values loyalty but is conflicted by the choices he must make to survive, Harry's journey is one of moral compromise. As the stakes escalate, Harry faces increasingly difficult decisions that call into question his commitment to both the Harrigan family and his own personal integrity.

2. Eddie Harrigan's Reckless Ambition: Eddie's storyline serves as both a catalyst for the central conflict and a reflection of the generational differences within the crime world. His impulsiveness leads to disastrous consequences for the Harrigans, but it also highlights the deeper issues within the family, particularly the tension between the old guard (Conrad and Maeve) and the younger generation (represented by Eddie). His arc explores themes of legacy, ambition, and the dangerous allure of power.

3. Conrad and Maeve Harrigan's Power Struggle: The power dynamic between Conrad and Maeve provides another rich narrative thread throughout the series. As

leaders of the Harrigan family, their relationship is defined by manipulation, secrecy, and a shared commitment to protecting the family business at any cost. However, their different approaches to leadership cause constant friction, leading to decisions that ultimately jeopardize the family's future.

4. The Rival Stevenson Family: The Stevensons are portrayed as a cold, calculating adversary to the Harrigans, with Richard Stevenson as the family's powerful and merciless leader. The Stevensons' role in the plot is not merely to serve as antagonists but as a mirror to the Harrigans' own internal struggles. Both families must confront their vulnerabilities, flaws, and secrets if they are to survive the escalating war.

5. External Threats: As the conflict between the two families intensifies, external threats begin to emerge in the form of law enforcement and rival crime syndicates. The presence of these outside forces serves to heighten the tension within the story, making it clear that the Harrigan and Stevenson families cannot continue their power struggles without consequence.

Analysis of Themes Explored in the Show

MobLand delves into several thematic areas, each adding depth and complexity to the overall narrative. Central themes include:

Family Loyalty: At the heart of the series is the question of what it means to be loyal to one's family. The Harrigans and Stevensons are driven by their allegiance to their respective families, yet each character's version of loyalty is tested in different ways. The series explores whether loyalty is a virtue or a liability, and what it costs to remain true to one's bloodline.

Crime and Power: MobLand examines the intersection of crime and power, exploring how individuals and families navigate their relationships with authority and the criminal underworld. The series critiques the idea of power as both a tool for survival and a destructive force. The characters' obsession with power ultimately leads to their downfall, highlighting the dangerous consequences of unchecked ambition.

Legacy and Succession: Both the Harrigans and the Stevensons are concerned with legacy—whether it's maintaining control of their criminal empires or passing them down to the next generation. The show explores how legacy shapes decisions and motivates actions, often resulting in the manipulation of younger family members to serve the family's greater goals.

Morality and Corruption: The moral ambiguity of the characters is one of the show's most compelling aspects. Each character, from the most ruthless crime boss to the seemingly innocent outsider, is faced with ethical dilemmas that challenge their sense of right and wrong. MobLand asks viewers to consider where morality fits into a world defined by crime, betrayal, and survival.

Comparison with Other Crime Dramas in the Genre

In terms of its narrative structure and thematic focus, MobLand draws clear parallels to other notable crime dramas. Like The Sopranos, it examines the emotional and psychological toll of living in the criminal underworld. However, MobLand distinguishes itself by placing greater emphasis on family dynamics and the personal struggles of its characters, rather than focusing solely on the action-driven elements of crime.

Additionally, MobLand shares similarities with Breaking Bad in its portrayal of a man grappling with his own moral descent. However, while Breaking Bad explores the transformation of an individual into a criminal mastermind, MobLand centers around a family—suggesting that the corruption of a family empire is a shared experience, not the singular downfall of one man.

While comparisons to other crime dramas are inevitable, MobLand brings a fresh perspective by weaving together character-driven storytelling, high-stakes crime, and the exploration of generational conflict. Its ability to balance these elements within a tightly woven narrative positions it as a standout in the genre, capturing the attention of both long-time crime drama fans and those seeking a more nuanced take on the genre.

Chapter 3: The Characters and Performances

Detailed Profiles of Main Characters

1. Harry Da Souza – The Fixer and Moral Center

Harry Da Souza, portrayed by Tom Hardy, is at the heart of MobLand. A seasoned fixer for the Harrigan family, Harry is a man of complex moral inclinations. He serves as the go-between for the family and the outside world, solving problems quietly, efficiently, and often without drawing attention. While his job demands ruthless pragmatism, Harry's character is defined by a subtle but intense internal struggle—he is deeply loyal to the Harrigan family, yet this loyalty is increasingly tested by the growing ethical dilemmas he faces.

Harry's journey throughout the series is one of self-discovery and moral reckoning. Hardy plays Harry with a brooding intensity, using his customary understated yet raw emotional range. While Harry is initially portrayed as a silent enforcer, Hardy skillfully unearths layers of vulnerability and conflict in his character, making him one of the most compelling figures in the show. The complexity of his character is brought to the forefront as he navigates the treacherous waters between professional duty and personal values.

His relationships with other characters, especially with Conrad and Maeve Harrigan, evolve over time, reflecting his shifting loyalties and the moral compromises that accompany his work.

2. Conrad Harrigan – The Patriarch and Power Broker

Played by Pierce Brosnan, Conrad Harrigan is the hardened patriarch of the Harrigan crime family. Conrad's character is a study in control, power, and pragmatism. A man who has spent decades at the helm of a vast criminal empire, Conrad views loyalty as a commodity, always weighing its cost and benefit. His leadership is marked by cold calculation and a deep sense of obligation to preserve the family legacy at all costs. However, beneath the surface, there are cracks in his armor—moments of vulnerability that hint at a man wrestling with his own fear of obsolescence.

Brosnan's portrayal of Conrad is both commanding and nuanced. As a seasoned actor, Brosnan brings an air of gravitas to the role, underscored by an innate sophistication that suggests Conrad's decades of criminal experience. He plays Conrad with a careful balance of charm and menace, effortlessly shifting between being a calculating mastermind and a vulnerable old man trying to maintain control of an empire that is slipping from his grasp. Conrad's complex relationship with his family, particularly with his wife

Maeve and grandson Eddie, is integral to the narrative, with Brosnan's performance highlighting the emotional distance and occasional affection that complicates these connections.

3. Maeve Harrigan – The Matriarch and Strategist

Maeve Harrigan, portrayed by Helen Mirren, is one of the most compelling figures in MobLand. As the matriarch of the Harrigan family, Maeve's character is a master strategist who wields power not just through brute force but through manipulation and emotional intelligence. She is a sharp, calculating woman who uses her wit and charm to control the people around her, and her role within the family dynamic is essential to maintaining order. While Conrad may be the face of the family's leadership, it is Maeve who often pulls the strings from the shadows.

Mirren brings a fierce, unrelenting energy to Maeve, capturing both her cold-blooded nature and her ability to maintain an emotional grip on the people around her. Unlike Conrad, Maeve does not shy away from using psychological tactics to manipulate her family and associates. Mirren's portrayal is marked by an incredible depth of emotion, allowing her to seamlessly navigate from moments of vulnerability to acts of calculated cruelty. As the story unfolds, Maeve's loyalty to her family is revealed to be as complicated and fraught with contradictions as the loyalty of those around her. Mirren's performance is both commanding and deeply human, making Maeve a character whose motivations are always compelling and never entirely predictable.

4. Eddie Harrigan – The Reckless Heir

Eddie Harrigan, the impulsive and often reckless grandson of Conrad and Maeve, serves as a catalyst for much of the conflict in MobLand. Played by a younger actor, Eddie is introduced as the heir to the family empire, but his brashness and youthful desire for power put him at odds with the older, more calculating figures in the family. Eddie's journey is one of self-discovery, as he seeks to prove himself worthy of his family's legacy, often making decisions that threaten not only his position within the family but the stability of the Harrigan empire itself.

Eddie is a character defined by his ambition and impulsiveness, traits that often lead him into dangerous situations. His relationship with Harry, as well as with his grandfather Conrad, is a study in generational conflict. Eddie sees himself as capable of leading the family, but his recklessness and inability to fully understand the weight of his actions position him as an unlikely successor. Eddie's character arc, marked by mistakes and self-destructive behavior, provides an emotional counterpoint to the older, more experienced characters around him.

Actor Performances and Character Development

The strength of MobLand lies in its exceptional cast and the depth they bring to their roles. Each actor in the central ensemble brings a level of complexity to their character that elevates the show above standard genre fare. The performances of Hardy, Brosnan, Mirren, and the supporting cast are key to the show's success, as each actor is able to create multidimensional characters whose motivations and desires are not immediately clear.

Tom Hardy's portrayal of Harry Da Souza is a testament to his ability to convey both inner conflict and quiet intensity. Hardy uses subtle gestures and restrained dialogue to communicate Harry's evolving sense of moral doubt, making the character's internal struggle palpable to the audience. This performance stands in contrast to Hardy's often more physically demanding roles, allowing him to show his versatility as an actor capable of capturing vulnerability as much as power.

Pierce Brosnan's turn as Conrad Harrigan is equally compelling. Known for playing charming yet dangerous characters, Brosnan brings a sense of menace to Conrad that is both calculated and chilling. His ability to present Conrad's internal battle—his desire to protect his legacy versus his fear of losing control—adds significant weight to the character's arc. Brosnan's nuanced approach to the role allows Conrad to emerge as a sympathetic yet morally ambiguous figure, highlighting the difficult choices faced by those in power.

Helen Mirren's Maeve is a masterclass in performance. Mirren's portrayal of the matriarch is a blend of elegance, sharp intellect, and ruthless pragmatism. Her commanding presence on screen anchors the show, and her ability to switch between icy detachment and emotional vulnerability makes Maeve one of the most unpredictable and captivating characters. Through Mirren's performance, Maeve emerges not just as a leader but as a woman who is constantly negotiating her identity within a patriarchal family structure.

Eddie Harrigan, played by a rising young actor, serves as the emotional heart of the younger generation's rebellion against the established order. His performance captures the impulsiveness and naïveté of youth, yet also conveys the pain of being part of a powerful family with expectations that are almost impossible to meet. As Eddie's character arc unfolds, his relationship with Harry becomes central to his development, with the older fixer acting as both mentor and adversary.

Behind-the-Scenes Insights from Interviews with Cast Members

In interviews with the cast, it became clear that the actors' relationships with their characters were deeply personal. Tom Hardy, in particular, expressed a deep understanding of Harry's internal conflict, explaining that the character's struggle was one that resonated with him on a personal level. "Harry is a man who wants to do good but finds himself trapped in a world where doing good isn't always an option," Hardy shared in an interview. This insight gave context to Hardy's nuanced performance, as he worked to bring out the quiet sorrow that defines Harry's character.

Pierce Brosnan, too, spoke about the complexities of playing Conrad Harrigan, noting that the role required him to balance Conrad's public persona as a powerful crime lord with his internal struggles as a father and grandfather. Brosnan admitted that portraying a character with such a morally gray outlook was challenging but ultimately rewarding. "Conrad is a man who has built his empire on ruthless decisions. What's interesting is that his love for his family complicates everything. It's not just about power; it's about fear of losing everything he's worked for," he said.

Helen Mirren, in discussing Maeve Harrigan, reflected on the challenges of portraying a female character in a traditionally male-dominated world of organized crime. She emphasized the importance of portraying Maeve as a multifaceted character, one who is both powerful and deeply human. "Maeve is a woman who has learned how to survive in a man's world. But underneath that toughness, there's a vulnerability. She loves her family, but she also knows that love can be a weapon," Mirren explained.

These behind-the-scenes insights highlight the depth of thought and preparation the actors brought to their roles, enhancing the authenticity of their performances and ensuring that each character was grounded in a believable emotional reality.

How Each Actor Fits into the Overall Narrative

Each actor in MobLand plays a crucial role in driving the narrative forward. Tom Hardy's Harry is central to the series' moral questions and character dynamics. His presence anchors the viewer's emotional connection to the story, and as the plot unfolds, his internal conflicts mirror the external chaos created by the war between the two families. Hardy's ability to convey subtlety and emotional depth brings a sense of realism to Harry's journey, making him one of the most engaging characters on screen.

Pierce Brosnan's Conrad, with his sharp mind and chilling decision-making, provides the stability needed for the series to explore its themes of power and legacy. His relationship with Maeve adds another layer of intrigue to the family dynamics, and Brosnan's performance ensures that Conrad remains a fascinating yet formidable character.

Helen Mirren's Maeve is perhaps the most dynamic and unpredictable character in the show. Her ability to manipulate, control, and care for her family in equal measure makes her a captivating presence in every scene. Mirren's portrayal of Maeve enriches the overall narrative by providing a counterbalance to the male characters, showing that power is not just about brute force, but about emotional intelligence and strategic thinking.

Lastly, Eddie Harrigan, portrayed by the young actor, represents the dangerous ambition of youth within the criminal world. His impulsiveness and desire to prove himself to his elders inject a sense of urgency and chaos into the family drama, making him a key figure in the narrative's progression.

Together, these characters create a complex, multifaceted portrayal of family and crime, ensuring that MobLand offers a compelling, layered storytelling experience. Each actor's performance contributes to the overall narrative arc, with their individual character developments intertwining to create a tense, high-stakes drama that is both thrilling and emotionally resonant.

Chapter 4: Production and Filming

Production Process: From Scripting to Shooting

The journey of MobLand from concept to screen was a meticulous process, spanning over a year of development, scripting, and pre-production work before the cameras began rolling in early 2024. While the idea for the series was initially conceived in 2023, the real work began when Guy Ritchie was brought in as director and executive producer, bringing with him his trademark style and an ambitious vision for the project. The production team quickly set to work on developing the scripts, which would serve as the foundation for the show's intricate narrative.

The writers and producers, under Ritchie's guidance, focused heavily on creating rich, multi-layered characters and a compelling story. This was not merely a procedural crime drama, but a complex tale of family, power, and moral ambiguity. The writers' room worked closely with Ritchie to ensure that each character's motivations and arcs were thoughtfully developed, allowing for deep emotional engagement from viewers. The dialogue in MobLand is sharp and laden with subtext, a hallmark of Ritchie's influence, reflecting the tension between loyalty and betrayal, ambition and familial duty.

Once the scripts were finalized, the production team moved into the pre-production phase. Casting was one of the earliest and most critical decisions, as the right actors were needed to bring the characters to life authentically. With the main cast secured—Tom Hardy, Pierce Brosnan, Helen Mirren, and others—the production crew began working on the logistics of filming, including choosing locations, designing sets, and planning the shoot's technical aspects.

Filming began in early 2024, with Ritchie closely involved in every step of the process. Ritchie is known for his hands-on approach to filmmaking, often involving himself in the day-to-day decisions on set. His meticulous attention to detail ensured that the tone and pacing of each scene matched the vision he had for the series. The directors and cinematographers worked collaboratively with him, ensuring that each shot was carefully framed to emphasize the emotional weight of the story.

Location Choices and Set Design

The choice of location was crucial in MobLand's production, as the setting plays a key role in conveying the gritty, tense atmosphere of the series. Though the show is set in a fictional urban environment, the production team chose to film in a series of diverse locations that allowed them to represent the multifaceted world of organized crime and family power. The decision to shoot in various parts of Europe—particularly in London and a few other major cities—gave the show a sense of authenticity while also providing a broader backdrop for the narrative.

The London streets, with their historical depth and industrial aesthetic, provided a fitting canvas for the series' tone. The city's combination of modernity and traditional architecture mirrored the story's blend of old-world crime and new-age power struggles. The bustling, gritty neighborhoods were used to evoke the rough, real-world setting in which the characters operate. From shadowy alleyways to expensive penthouses, the locations captured the divide between the luxurious world of the Harrigan family and the harsh, brutal reality of the streets they control.

In addition to the exterior shots, a significant portion of the filming took place on meticulously designed sets that created the feeling of claustrophobia and isolation. The interiors of the Harrigan family's mansion, for example, were designed with great attention to detail, using a mix of opulent yet worn-down elements that conveyed both the wealth of the crime empire and the inherent decay within the family. The set design was intended to reflect the characters' complex relationships and the personal stakes at play in each scene. The contrast between cold, sterile boardrooms and the warmth of intimate family spaces emphasized the dual nature of the show's narrative.

Directorial Style of Guy Ritchie and Its Impact on the Series

Guy Ritchie's directorial style is one of the defining aspects of MobLand. Known for his fast-paced, visually striking storytelling, Ritchie brings a level of energy and sophistication to the series that sets it apart from many other crime dramas. His background in film—particularly with crime films like Lock, Stock and Two Smoking Barrels and Snatch—informs his approach to MobLand, yet his decision to adapt his style for a long-form television series was both innovative and bold.

One of Ritchie's signature techniques is the use of nonlinear storytelling, where events unfold out of sequence or through multiple perspectives. In MobLand, this technique is employed to great effect, creating a sense of mystery and tension as the audience is gradually fed information about the characters and their motives. This allows Ritchie to build suspense, dropping subtle clues that deepen the intrigue as the show progresses. His style ensures that the viewer is always engaged, constantly working to piece together the various storylines and characters' motivations.

Another hallmark of Ritchie's work is his ability to balance sharp, witty dialogue with moments of intense violence and drama. While MobLand certainly contains its share of action, Ritchie does not rely on physical confrontation alone to drive the story forward. Instead, he focuses on the characters' psychological battles—using dialogue, atmosphere, and small, powerful moments to create tension. The show's pacing reflects this approach, with Ritchie orchestrating the flow of scenes to keep the viewer on edge without overwhelming them with spectacle.

Ritchie's attention to character development and emotional depth is also a crucial element of MobLand. He approached the actors as collaborators, encouraging them to delve deep into their roles and find subtle nuances that would add layers to their performances. This method gave rise to a series that is not just about crime, but about the personal cost of living a life defined by crime and power.

Challenges During Filming and How They Were Overcome

As with any large-scale production, MobLand faced its fair share of challenges during filming. One of the most significant obstacles was the logistics of shooting in various locations, particularly in urban areas that were often difficult to access. The production team had to navigate the complexities of filming in busy city streets, ensuring minimal disruption to the public while maintaining the cinematic look and feel of the scenes. The weather also posed a challenge, particularly when filming on location during the colder months in London. Rain and cold temperatures slowed down certain exterior shots, and filming had to be paused on multiple occasions to wait for the right conditions.

The size of the production itself also presented logistical issues. With a large ensemble cast, intricate sets, and numerous action sequences, managing the coordination between departments (camera, lighting, sound, etc.) required precise planning. Ritchie and the producers worked closely with the crew to ensure that each scene was shot efficiently and within the budget, without sacrificing the quality of the final product.

Additionally, MobLand features several action sequences and stunt-heavy moments that required detailed choreography and expert coordination. These scenes, which often involve close combat or tense shootouts, demanded careful planning to ensure safety while still delivering the thrilling spectacle expected from a crime drama. The stunt coordinators worked alongside Ritchie to design sequences that would both satisfy action fans and contribute to the overall story, rather than detracting from it.

The nature of MobLand's narrative also posed unique challenges in terms of pacing and tension. With its complex characters and intricate subplots, the story needed to maintain a careful balance between moments of high intensity and quieter, more reflective scenes. Ritchie, known for his sharp editing style, worked closely with the editors to ensure that each episode maintained the right balance between action, drama, and character development. The series is edited to be fast-paced yet focused, allowing the viewer to remain engaged while fully appreciating the depth of the character interactions.

Notable Technical Achievements

One of the standout features of MobLand is its exceptional technical execution, with particular attention paid to cinematography, sound design, and the overall visual aesthetic of the series. The cinematography, led by renowned Director of Photography (DP) John Mathieson, was a key aspect of the show's visual identity. Mathieson, who previously worked with Ritchie on RocknRolla and Sherlock Holmes, brought a cinematic flair to the series. The camera work is deliberate and expressive, using a mix of wide shots to capture the scale of the criminal empire and close-ups to convey the emotional intensity of key moments.

The use of light and shadow is one of the series' most notable technical achievements. The lighting design plays a significant role in shaping the tone of the series, with dark, moody lighting used in the interiors of the Harrigan family estate and harsh, cold lighting in scenes that depict the brutality of the criminal underworld. This contrast highlights the moral ambiguity of the characters, suggesting that even in the most opulent surroundings, there is a sense of decay and danger lurking just beneath the surface.

The sound design of MobLand is equally impressive, contributing to the immersive atmosphere of the series.

The score, composed by the talented Daniel Pemberton, uses a mix of modern and classical elements to evoke both the contemporary setting and the timeless nature of the themes at play. The music is carefully woven into the narrative, underscoring moments of tension and release. Pemberton's score is both haunting and powerful, ensuring that the emotional beats of the show resonate with the audience.

Additionally, the sound mixing and sound effects work to heighten the realism of the action sequences. From the sounds of gunfire in intense standoffs to the subtle creaking of the family's mansion, the attention to auditory detail helps create an atmosphere of unease and anticipation. The sound design is critical in maintaining the series' overall tone, seamlessly blending with the cinematography to heighten the emotional impact of each scene.

Together, the cinematography, sound, and visual design of MobLand create a distinctive aesthetic that enhances the storytelling and deepens the viewer's engagement with the world of the show. The technical achievements of the series not only highlight the skill of the production team but also serve to elevate MobLand beyond the typical crime drama, making it a standout example of quality television.

Chapter 5: Critical Reception

Reviews from Critics Across Major Publications

Upon its release, MobLand sparked a notable divide among critics. While some lauded its cinematic ambition and commanding performances, others raised concerns about its reliance on familiar genre structures. Across major review aggregators, the initial numbers painted a picture of cautious admiration.

On Rotten Tomatoes, MobLand debuted with a 71% approval rating based on 14 critic reviews. The critical consensus noted the show's atmospheric direction and powerful performances, particularly from Tom Hardy and Helen Mirren, but also cited pacing issues in early episodes. Metacritic offered a more tempered reception, assigning the show a score of 57 out of 100, indicating "mixed or average reviews." These early metrics suggested a show with clear strengths but also elements that divided opinion.

The New York Times described MobLand as "moody, stylish, and fiercely acted," while also pointing out that its plot at times "leans too heavily on genre tropes without offering sufficient subversion." The Guardian was more enthusiastic, calling it "Guy Ritchie's best work in years," highlighting his evolution from stylized action to more emotionally grounded storytelling. In contrast, The Atlantic criticized the series for its lack of novelty, claiming it "offers finely crafted scenes in service of well-worn themes."

Trade publications took a more analytical view. Variety praised the show's production quality and score but raised concerns about narrative cohesion. "The technical artistry is undeniable," one review noted, "but the story occasionally meanders, particularly in the middle episodes." The Hollywood Reporter commended the casting and visual design but felt the character development of secondary figures lagged behind the central trio.

Across these early assessments, a pattern emerged: critics were largely united in their respect for the show's craft and acting, but opinions varied on whether MobLand offered enough innovation to distinguish itself from its genre peers.

Audience Reactions and Feedback

Viewer responses to MobLand presented a markedly different picture. Audience engagement was robust from the first episode, particularly among viewers already familiar with Guy Ritchie's previous work. Social media activity surged in the days following the premiere, with hashtags related to the series trending globally. Audience-driven platforms reflected stronger sentiment than critic-based sites: on IMDb, MobLand secured a 7.9/10 rating in its first two weeks, based on several thousand user reviews. On Letterboxd, commentary often emphasized admiration for the acting and atmosphere, with many praising its "slow-burn" intensity.

User reviews on Rotten Tomatoes offered more positive reactions than those of critics. Many cited Tom Hardy's portrayal of Harry Da Souza as a standout, praising the quiet emotional gravity he brought to a role that could easily have become one-note. One viewer wrote, "Tom Hardy delivers one of his most layered performances. He makes you believe in Harry's internal war without ever saying much."

Helen Mirren's role as Maeve Harrigan also drew frequent praise. Many fans were struck by the strength and unpredictability of her character. "She owns every scene," one fan remarked on Reddit. "Not your stereotypical crime matriarch—she's colder, sharper, and somehow more human."

On the other hand, a subset of viewers expressed dissatisfaction with the show's pace. Some felt the first three episodes were overly dense, prioritizing atmosphere over plot development. "I almost gave up after episode two," one viewer tweeted, "but glad I stayed. It finally kicks into gear around episode four."

Fan engagement extended beyond episodic reactions. The series inspired breakdown videos on YouTube, character analysis threads on forums, and speculative fan theories—especially surrounding the ambiguous motivations of several key characters. The show's narrative density and morally grey characters fueled discussions that helped sustain interest between episodes.

Analysis of the Show's Impact on the Crime Drama Genre

Though still early in its run, MobLand has already begun to shape conversations about the direction of modern crime drama. While its foundational elements—organized crime, intergenerational conflict, morally conflicted anti-heroes—are genre staples, the show's presentation of these elements reflects evolving viewer expectations.

Critics and scholars have noted the show's emphasis on introspection over action. In contrast to the propulsive violence of series like Peaky Blinders or Boardwalk Empire, MobLand often pauses for moral ambiguity and emotional weight. This shift toward quieter storytelling, underscored by long silences, tightly framed interiors, and reflective dialogue, marks a departure from the fast-cut montages that defined earlier Ritchie projects.

The series has also contributed to a reimagining of traditional power dynamics within crime families. Maeve Harrigan, for instance, is not simply a supportive wife or background presence. Her role as co-strategist within the Harrigan empire invites comparisons to Carmela Soprano or Gemma Teller, but unlike those figures, Maeve operates with overt authority. Her character challenges longstanding genre conventions that often sideline female figures in organized crime narratives.

Additionally, MobLand reflects a broader trend in prestige television: a move away from traditional arcs toward episodic character studies. Each installment focuses as much on revealing internal motivations as it does on advancing plot. This approach aligns it more closely with recent series like Tokyo Vice or ZeroZeroZero, which emphasize character psychology within structurally complex criminal ecosystems.

As MobLand continues its run, industry analysts are watching to see whether its approach influences the next wave of crime dramas—particularly those in development at streaming platforms, where creative risks are more often rewarded.

Comparisons to Other Crime-Themed Series or Films

MobLand has drawn inevitable comparisons to some of the most iconic crime dramas of the past two decades. In its focus on family legacy and moral erosion, the show invites parallels with The Sopranos. Yet, unlike David Chase's psychological deep-dive into Tony Soprano's psyche, MobLand spreads its emotional inquiry across multiple characters, especially Harry, Maeve, and Conrad. This ensemble focus distinguishes it from character-centric dramas and reflects a more fragmented, postmodern narrative structure.

Guy Ritchie's influence also places MobLand in conversation with his own cinematic work. However, while Lock, Stock and Two Smoking Barrels and Snatch leaned into kinetic storytelling and stylized editing, MobLand exercises more restraint. The show forgoes ironic narration and visual gags in favor of methodical tension-building and thematic weight. This tonal shift has drawn comparisons to The Godfather trilogy—particularly in the interplay between personal ambition and family duty—though MobLand avoids overt homage.

Other comparisons have been made to Peaky Blinders, particularly in terms of visual composition and the centrality of power struggles within a tightly controlled criminal structure. Yet where Peaky Blinders romanticized its historical setting and protagonist, MobLand resists glamorizing any part of its world. It is less operatic, more psychological.

Streaming platforms have also prompted comparisons to international titles like Gomorrah and Suburra, both of which offer a bleak, hyper-realistic view of organized crime. MobLand, while similarly serious in tone, integrates a more intimate emotional register, making its moral inquiries feel less abstract and more grounded in the personal stakes of its characters.

Controversies or Debates Surrounding the Series

Despite its overall success, MobLand has not been without its controversies. The most notable debate centers on its depiction of violence. Several commentators have pointed to the show's stylized yet emotionally charged portrayals of brutality, questioning whether some scenes cross the line from necessary realism into gratuitous spectacle. In particular, a violent interrogation sequence in episode five drew criticism for its graphic nature, prompting online discussions about the ethics of violence in serialized storytelling.

Another point of contention has been the show's representation of ethnicity and class. While MobLand is set in a diverse urban environment, some critics have argued that its portrayal of non-white characters is limited, with few appearing in central roles. While the series doesn't rely on racial stereotypes, the relative lack of diversity among its lead characters has been noted in both critical essays and viewer forums.

Guy Ritchie, during press interviews, addressed these concerns by acknowledging the challenges of representation in crime narratives. "We were focused on telling a very specific family story," he stated. "But as the series progresses, there are plans to widen the scope of the world and introduce new characters that reflect a broader social reality."

There has also been academic debate about the show's thematic ambiguity. Some scholars argue that the show's refusal to clearly distinguish heroes from villains reflects the moral complexity of real life, while others believe this ambiguity can muddle viewer engagement, leaving audiences unclear about the show's ethical position.

In the public sphere, most viewer debates have centered less on moral themes and more on pacing. While many praised the slow-burn approach, others found the series' structure too deliberately paced, especially for a show marketed as a high-stakes crime drama. Discussions on Reddit and fan blogs frequently cite the first three episodes as divisive—some calling them "a masterclass in mood," others labeling them "an endurance test."

Despite these debates, MobLand has maintained its cultural momentum. Whether praised or critiqued, it has remained a topic of sustained discussion, a clear indicator of its relevance within the broader landscape of contemporary crime television.

Chapter 6: Cultural Impact

"MobLand" as Part of the Broader Trend in Crime Media

MobLand is part of a broader cultural phenomenon that has seen a resurgence of crime-based media in the past decade. The rise of high-quality crime dramas and thrillers, particularly in the television and streaming sectors, has captivated global audiences. MobLand, with its nuanced take on family dynamics, loyalty, and power struggles within organized crime, enters a market already populated by series like Breaking Bad, The Sopranos, and Narcos. However, the show's distinct approach—blending Guy Ritchie's unique directorial style with complex character studies—helps it stand apart from other crime dramas, adding a new layer to the evolving genre.

One key trend within modern crime media is the focus on the moral ambiguity of its central characters. Anti-heroes have become the hallmark of many successful crime series, and MobLand follows this pattern, offering viewers characters who are simultaneously relatable and repulsive. The duality of these characters, particularly in the form of Harry Da Souza (Tom Hardy) and Maeve Harrigan (Helen Mirren), taps into a cultural curiosity about the complexities of crime and punishment, family loyalty, and moral choice.

Additionally, the trend toward exploring organized crime as a multi-generational phenomenon is another theme MobLand shares with its predecessors. Much like The Sopranos explored the influence of family heritage on personal identity and behavior, MobLand delves into the burden of legacy within a crime family. This focus on legacy, power struggles, and the passing down of criminal empires reflects broader societal concerns about inheritance, power, and the entanglement of personal and professional lives in the context of systemic corruption.

Crime dramas are also increasingly popular because they often tap into a global fascination with the underworld. MobLand follows in the footsteps of Narcos, Peaky Blinders, and Gomorrah in presenting a world where law and order are elusive, and the boundaries of morality are constantly shifting. These shows, including MobLand, are indicative of a growing appetite for stories that present crime not merely as a set of illegal activities, but as a way of life—a means of survival, power, and personal validation.

How the Show Has Reshaped Global Audiences' Views on Crime and Power

On a global scale, MobLand has struck a chord with audiences interested in the darker undercurrents of criminal life. Crime dramas, especially those like MobLand that delve into organized crime, often highlight the systemic forces that shape individual actions within the context of larger power structures. In the case of MobLand, the battle between the Harrigan and Stevenson families illustrates the larger societal forces that drive individuals to make morally questionable decisions in order to maintain power or secure their futures.

For viewers, the series prompts reflection on how power—whether familial, corporate, or governmental—often perpetuates cycles of corruption and violence. As with many other crime dramas, MobLand invites audiences to consider the blurred lines between right and wrong. In this series, even characters that seem like villains—such as Conrad Harrigan or Richard Stevenson—are painted with shades of gray, forcing viewers to question whether they are the product of an unjust system or agents of their own destiny.

The show has also resonated with global audiences by tapping into a collective fascination with the mafia genre. In countries like Italy, where organized crime has been an ongoing issue for decades, MobLand is both a reflection of and a commentary on the influence of crime families in shaping society. Similarly, in North America, where media portrayals of the mafia and organized crime have been staple genres for decades, MobLand offers a fresh embrace.

The show's focus on the Harrigan family, spanning multiple generations, allows for an exploration of power structures, legacy, and generational conflict—common themes in recent crime media. While earlier crime dramas often centered around singular figures of authority or rebellion (e.g., Tony Soprano or Walter White), MobLand enriches this narrative by focusing on the familial and generational conflicts within the crime world, a perspective that has gained prominence in recent television.

Another significant trend MobLand taps into is the rise of streaming platforms as the primary venue for high-budget, high-quality crime dramas. In an era where traditional networks often struggle to match the cinematic quality of content on services like Netflix, Amazon Prime, and Paramount+, MobLand benefits from the freedom these platforms offer. The creative liberties and longer, episodic format available on platforms like Paramount+ allow for a more intricate exploration of character motivations and complex storylines that might not fit the typical constraints of network television.

With its finely detailed character arcs, morally complex narrative, and visually stunning production, MobLand contributes to this trend of crime dramas evolving into sophisticated pieces of storytelling that blur the lines between high art and popular entertainment.

How the Show Has Resonated with Global Audiences

Since its release, MobLand has resonated with a diverse, global audience. Crime dramas have long had international appeal, particularly those that explore universal themes of power, family, and betrayal. What sets MobLand apart, however, is its ability to tap into these themes with both modern relevance and historical depth, allowing it to connect with viewers around the world.

One factor contributing to the show's international appeal is its portrayal of familiar yet compelling characters. While the setting of MobLand is fictional, its characters embody archetypes that are universally recognized, such as the ambitious son, the ruthless patriarch, and the strategic matriarch. These figures, while operating within a specific crime family, represent broader themes of familial loyalty, ambition, and conflict that transcend cultural boundaries. Audiences across different continents can identify with the internal struggles and relational complexities portrayed in the show, whether through the lens of their own family dynamics or their understanding of generational conflict.

The show has also benefited from the global rise of streaming services. Paramount+, which offers MobLand to international markets, has made the series available to audiences beyond the United States, helping the show gain traction in markets such as the UK, Canada, and parts of Europe, Asia, and Latin America. By leveraging the accessibility of streaming, the show has been able to reach viewers who might not traditionally tune into network television or cable, solidifying its place as a global phenomenon.

In particular, MobLand's European locations and aesthetic appeal have contributed to its resonance across the continent. With its moody, urban settings and European-style cinematography, the series aligns with successful international crime dramas such as Gomorrah (Italy) and Sacred Games (India). These series have also explored complex criminal networks and their impact on society, and MobLand's thematic exploration of the familial side of crime has found a similar audience across cultures.

Beyond geographic reach, MobLand has been embraced by younger audiences who are increasingly turning to crime dramas that explore the psychological and emotional dimensions of criminal life. This shift, from purely action-driven narratives to more introspective character-driven stories, has been crucial in the show's appeal. Viewers in their 20s and 30s—who might have grown up with more traditional gangster films—are now seeking out complex stories that go beyond mere crime and delve into the personal costs of such a lifestyle.

The Influence of Crime Dramas on Societal Perceptions of Crime

Crime dramas like MobLand play a significant role in shaping public perception of crime, particularly organized crime. Over the decades, crime dramas have walked a fine line between glamorizing the criminal underworld and exploring its darker, more destructive realities. Shows like The Sopranos and Narcos helped reframe the way crime families are depicted, focusing less on their glorified exploits and more on the human cost of their actions. MobLand continues this trend by delving deeply into the moral ambiguities faced by its characters, encouraging viewers to reflect on the nature of crime and the price of power.

The portrayal of organized crime in MobLand invites audiences to consider how easily individuals can become entangled in systems of corruption, whether by family legacy, financial necessity, or ambition. The way the Harrigan family navigates its criminal empire is, at times, more a study of survival than a glorification of wealth and power. This nuanced depiction of crime underscores the tension between personal morality and survival instincts, showing how people justify their involvement in destructive behavior, often in the name of familial loyalty.

By humanizing its characters and showing their emotional and psychological conflicts, MobLand encourages viewers to consider the broader societal implications of organized crime—its effects not only on its perpetrators but also on their families, communities, and environments. The show indirectly critiques the systemic nature of criminal organizations, particularly how they feed off societal inequalities, and it underscores the personal costs of being involved in such systems. For audiences, this is not just an exploration of crime in a fictional sense, but a reflection on how power and corruption function in the real world.

Importantly, the show also touches on the societal factors that push people into criminal activities. By highlighting Harry Da Souza's struggle to reconcile his moral compass with the demands of his job as a fixer, MobLand highlights the complex reasons people turn to crime, including the pressures of loyalty, financial need, and the desire for power. These themes make the show an important cultural touchstone for discussions about justice, ethics, and the human condition.

Impact on the Careers of Actors and Filmmakers Involved

The release of MobLand has had a marked impact on the careers of its cast and crew, particularly Tom Hardy, Pierce Brosnan, and Helen Mirren. Tom Hardy's portrayal of Harry Da Souza has been widely praised, adding another nuanced performance to his already impressive repertoire. Known for his ability to play physically demanding and complex characters, Hardy's role in MobLand showcases his range as an actor, moving away from the action-heavy roles he is most associated with and embracing a more subtle, emotionally layered performance. This shift has only enhanced his reputation as one of Hollywood's most versatile actors.

Helen Mirren, too, has received widespread acclaim for her portrayal of Maeve Harrigan, one of the most compelling and unpredictable characters in the series. Her role in MobLand further solidifies her status as one of the most respected actresses of her generation. Mirren's portrayal of a female crime boss who wields power both through intellect and manipulation is a standout in a genre traditionally dominated by male figures. The role has sparked renewed interest in Mirren's ability to tackle complex, multi-dimensional characters, potentially opening the door for more prominent roles in similar genres.

Pierce Brosnan's turn as Conrad Harrigan marks a return to dramatic roles for the actor, having long been associated with lighter action films, most notably as James Bond. Brosnan's portrayal of a ruthless crime patriarch has earned him praise for his ability to balance menace and vulnerability, further expanding his range as an actor. His role in MobLand has been seen as a career-defining performance that showcases his ability to handle darker, more dramatic material.

Guy Ritchie's involvement in MobLand also marks a significant point in his career, particularly as it is his first foray into serialized television. Known for his success in the film industry, Ritchie's shift to television has proven to be a strategic move, allowing him to explore deeper, more complex stories over an extended format. The success of MobLand affirms Ritchie's ability to transition between mediums without losing his unique style and directorial vision. His work on the series has reinvigorated interest in his particular brand of storytelling, which combines fast-paced dialogue, dark humor, and complex characters.

Fan Culture, Memes, and Social Media Engagement

As with many successful modern series, MobLand has sparked an active fan culture that thrives on social media platforms like Twitter, Reddit, and Instagram. Fans of the show regularly engage in discussions about character motivations, plot twists, and the broader themes of the series. Memes about the show, often centered around the characters' iconic lines and moments of dark humor, quickly spread across social media, helping to keep the series in the public eye between episodes.

Reddit, in particular, has become a hub for in-depth analysis and fan theories. Users frequently post breakdowns of each episode, discussing character development, potential plotlines, and hidden details they believe Ritchie and his team have embedded in the show. The "MobLand" subreddit is filled with fan-generated content, from fan art to conspiracy theories about the show's future direction. This level of engagement indicates a deep connection between the audience and the series, suggesting that MobLand has resonated on an emotional and intellectual level with its viewers.

On Twitter, hashtags related to the show, such as #MobLand, #Harry D'Souza, and #MaeveHarrigan, trend after each new episode. Fans post their reactions in real-time, creating a sense of communal viewing, with users often tagging the actors and filmmakers in their tweets to express admiration for their work. The real-time interaction has helped the show maintain a significant presence in the social media landscape.

In addition to memes and online discussions, fan podcasts dedicated to MobLand have sprung up, with hosts dissecting each episode in minute detail and inviting listeners to contribute their own theories. These fan-driven platforms serve as an extension of the show's narrative, allowing audiences to engage in the story beyond just watching it unfold on-screen. This kind of fan culture has become a critical element in the show's success, ensuring it remains a topic of conversation long after the credits roll.

Overall, MobLand has created a vibrant and active fan base that extends far beyond its airing schedule, engaging viewers in a way that keeps the show relevant in a competitive media landscape. Social media has allowed MobLand to thrive in the digital age, turning its narrative into a cultural touchstone for discussions about power, crime, and the human experience.

Chapter 7: The Music and Soundtrack

Exploration of the Music Used in "MobLand"

The soundtrack of MobLand is not a background feature but an essential component of its narrative architecture. Composed by Daniel Pemberton, whose recent work in film (The Trial of the Chicago 7, Spider-Man: Into the Spider-Verse) has received critical acclaim, the music of MobLand combines modern sonic elements with classical instrumentation to create an immersive aural landscape. It avoids drawing attention to itself in obvious ways, instead embedding meaning and tension directly into the sonic structure of the series.

Pemberton's score is deliberately restrained, opting for mood and subtle tension over bombast. Much of the soundtrack employs low-register strings, ambient textures, and minor-key progressions that build unease rather than dictate emotion. This restraint mirrors the show's broader aesthetic: a quiet, slow-burning exploration of control, legacy, and psychological unraveling. Rather than rely on instantly recognizable motifs or grand orchestration, the music is organic and minimal, shaped to complement the emotional state of the characters rather than overpower them.

The series also incorporates curated diegetic music—songs playing from radios, record players, or within club scenes—that help anchor the narrative in a textured, lived-in world. The choices here are eclectic: vintage jazz, late-'90s trip-hop, ambient electronica, and British post-punk all make appearances. These selections reflect the layered identity of the world in which the Harrigan and Stevenson families operate: a modern criminal empire built on old foundations.

Music supervisors Jane Fitzgerald and Aaron Mottram worked closely with Pemberton and the showrunners to ensure that each piece of music aligned with the characters' environments, histories, and emotional states. Their selections avoid the expected. Instead of defaulting to genre clichés—such as opera during violent sequences or rap during chase scenes—MobLand uses music with restraint, offering sound as emotional punctuation rather than spectacle.

Role of the Soundtrack in Building Atmosphere

The atmosphere of MobLand is defined as much by what is heard as by what is seen. The music doesn't underscore the action in traditional ways. It seeps in at the edges, often playing against the visual tone to create an undercurrent of tension. In this way, the soundtrack behaves like an additional character—always present, always shaping how the viewer perceives the world on screen.

Scenes of negotiation and familial conflict are frequently accompanied by ambient soundscapes that feel almost industrial—metallic drones, echoes, and low-pitched mechanical hums. These elements amplify the emotional tension without directly telegraphing danger. In other moments, the music drops out entirely, allowing silence to take over. The absence of music becomes its own device, highlighting moments of emotional stillness or psychological collapse. In episode four, for example, during a key conversation between Harry Da Souza and Maeve Harrigan, the lack of any score draws attention to the rhythm of their voices, the weight of the pauses between words, and the strain in their expressions.

The soundtrack also helps delineate the spatial geography of the series. Different musical textures are used for different families and locations. The Harrigan household is often underscored with minimalist piano motifs and subdued strings, suggesting formality and control. In contrast, the Stevenson scenes lean into dissonant synthesizers and distorted bass lines, evoking chaos and volatility. These distinctions help viewers immediately feel the difference in atmosphere between scenes, even before any dialogue is spoken.

Lighting, production design, and cinematography often work in tandem with the music to enhance mood. When Maeve walks through the Harrigan estate's corridors at night, the music mirrors her measured steps with quiet rhythmic pulses, reinforcing her authority and the cold calculation of her decisions. These moments elevate the soundtrack from being merely supportive to fundamentally narrative in its function.

Analysis of Notable Musical Cues and Their Significance

Throughout the series, there are several recurring motifs and musical cues that carry narrative significance. One such motif—used sparingly but memorably—is a minor-key cello line associated with Harry Da Souza. It first appears in the pilot episode during a moment of introspection, as Harry watches his reflection in a cracked mirror. The motif returns in key scenes where Harry's moral uncertainty is foregrounded: during his reluctant participation in violence, his conversations with Conrad, and a pivotal moment at the end of episode six when he chooses not to act against a perceived threat.

This motif does not evolve in a traditional musical sense; it reappears nearly unchanged, serving as a sonic marker of Harry's psychological stasis. The repetition suggests his inability to move forward emotionally, even as the circumstances around him become increasingly volatile. It's a musical encapsulation of his inner paralysis.

Another cue worth noting is the choral motif used during scenes involving Maeve Harrigan. Unlike Harry's motif, Maeve's is grander—though still understated—featuring layered female vocals that blend traditional harmonies with unsettling overtones. This cue accompanies her scenes of strategic manipulation, adding a sense of mythic detachment to her character. It frames her not just as a matriarch but as a near-oracular force within the narrative. The choice to use vocals, especially layered voices, is significant—it suggests both command and distance, as if Maeve exists above the emotional fray, orchestrating events from an elevated vantage point.

The Stevenson family, by contrast, is not given a singular musical motif but is represented through fragmented, dissonant sounds—an intentional lack of musical cohesion that mirrors the family's more chaotic and impulsive energy. These textures become more prevalent as the Stevenson-Harrigan conflict intensifies. A sharp, looping percussive element—first heard during a botched deal in episode three—reappears in altered forms throughout the season, acting as an auditory signal of rising instability within the criminal landscape.

There are also moments in MobLand where music serves to reframe a scene's emotional tone. In episode eight, during a particularly brutal confrontation, a mellow acoustic track plays in the background—an unexpected contrast to the on-screen violence. This juxtaposition does not soften the impact but intensifies it, highlighting the senselessness of the moment and drawing attention to the emotional numbness of the characters involved. Such choices reflect a deliberate subversion of genre expectations, where music is not used to validate the viewer's emotional reaction but to complicate it.

How Music Contributes to the Overall Storytelling

The role of music in MobLand is not limited to mood-setting. It also serves as a narrative tool, conveying information about characters, themes, and emotional undercurrents that might not be fully articulated through dialogue or visuals. In a show where silence and subtext are as important as spoken word, music provides a vital third layer of meaning.

The musical choices across the season function almost like an internal monologue for the show's characters. Rather than underscore external action, the soundtrack more often reflects internal states—guilt, resolve, anxiety, fear. These emotional cues help guide the audience's interpretation of ambiguous scenes, particularly in a series where characters often mask their true feelings. When Harry walks away from a crime scene, his face unreadable, the swelling of dissonant strings lets the viewer into his psychological state. In this way, music becomes a narrative device—revealing what characters conceal.

The soundtrack also reinforces thematic continuity across episodes. Themes of repetition, inevitability, and entrapment—central to the narrative—are mirrored in the music's cyclical structures. Repeated motifs, slight variations, and unresolved harmonies create a sonic environment that mirrors the characters' inability to escape their roles within the family or the criminal world.

These musical patterns become more insistent as the series progresses, subtly reflecting the tightening grip of fate on the main characters.

Crucially, music in MobLand never insists on a singular emotional reading. Instead, it leaves space for interpretation. The ambiguity in the score—its refusal to resolve harmonically, its embrace of tonal dissonance—mirrors the show's narrative ambiguity. In a series defined by blurred moral lines and unstable alliances, the music resists offering clear emotional guidance. It does not tell the audience how to feel; it invites them to sit with uncertainty.

Beyond its emotional resonance, the music helps shape pacing. Episodes of MobLand tend to alternate between slow, dialogue-heavy scenes and sudden bursts of action. The soundtrack helps bridge these tonal shifts, providing a sense of cohesion even as the narrative pivots. In scenes of transition—between storylines, locations, or emotional beats—music acts as connective tissue, maintaining narrative flow and grounding the viewer in the show's evolving mood.

In MobLand, music is neither ornamental nor auxiliary. It is part of the storytelling infrastructure—a carefully constructed system of motifs, textures, and cues that provide depth and nuance to an already rich narrative world. As the series continues, the evolving relationship between score and story promises to remain one of its most quietly powerful elements.

Chapter 8: Future of the Series

Possible Directions for Future Seasons (Based on Fan Theories and Hints from Creators)

As MobLand continues to build its fanbase and generate intense interest, speculation about its future is rampant. The series, with its intricate plotlines and morally complex characters, leaves plenty of room for further development in subsequent seasons. Based on both fan theories and hints from the creators, several possible directions for future seasons are emerging.

One of the most discussed fan theories centers around the continued moral descent of Harry Da Souza. As the series progresses, Harry's internal conflict between loyalty to the Harrigan family and his desire for a more peaceful life becomes increasingly fraught. Fans speculate that the next season could explore Harry's decision to finally break away from the criminal world. This potential arc could see Harry either turning against the Harrigans entirely or—more dramatically—becoming an unwitting ally to the rival Stevenson family. Such a shift could bring him into direct conflict with the people he has long considered family, opening the door for significant character growth and moral ambiguity.

There are also hints within the series that suggest the fractured Harrigan family will remain at the center of future seasons, with more in-depth exploration of the power struggles between Conrad and Maeve. As the show moves forward, viewers may see the increasing strain in their relationship, particularly as the younger generation (specifically Eddie) looks to assert himself. Conrad's old-school approach to crime and leadership may clash with Maeve's more calculated, manipulative tactics. The tension between the two could become a central conflict, driving not only the family dynamic but also the criminal empire's future.

On the other side, MobLand has hinted at introducing fresh external forces into the narrative, potentially in the form of law enforcement or rival gangs. One theory involves the arrival of a federal agent with a personal vendetta against the Harrigans. This could create an exciting new layer of tension as the Harrigans try to keep their criminal empire intact while evading the law. Such a storyline could push the characters into even more desperate and morally questionable actions.

The most recent season also introduced a number of characters whose backstories remain shrouded in mystery. The introduction of an unknown associate of Maeve Harrigan, for instance, has sparked speculation about a hidden network of allies and enemies who could play larger roles in upcoming seasons. Fans are particularly intrigued by the possibility that certain side characters, like the enigmatic fixer who works for the Stevensons, may have secret ties to the Harrigan family or could represent a future threat.

The direction of MobLand's second season will likely hinge on its ability to maintain the slow-burn character development that has kept its audience engaged while ramping up the stakes in both personal and professional conflicts. The balance between the family drama and external threats, combined with the evolving dynamics among the main characters, will be key to sustaining interest moving forward.

Speculation About New Characters or Plotlines

As MobLand continues to evolve, the introduction of new characters and plotlines is almost certain. One anticipated development is the possible rise of new power players, particularly from outside the Harrigan and Stevenson families. Given the global appeal of organized crime dramas, it's plausible that future seasons could explore international connections, with new figures from Eastern Europe, the Middle East, or even South America entering the fray. These new characters could introduce fresh challenges for the established families, whether in the form of ruthless mercenaries, corrupt businessmen, or rival crime syndicates seeking to establish their own foothold.

Additionally, fan speculation points to the possibility of a larger focus on the world of illegal business operations beyond traditional organized crime. In previous episodes, there were brief mentions of money laundering, human trafficking, and cybercrime. Future seasons could see the Harrigans expanding their operations to meet the demands of a modern, digital criminal landscape. This shift could introduce new characters in the tech or finance sectors, further diversifying the criminal ecosystem in which the series takes place.

On the character front, many fans expect the return of certain secondary characters who have only appeared in a limited capacity thus far. Characters like the ambitious, yet reckless, Eddie Harrigan could be positioned as a more prominent figure in future seasons. Eddie's arc could evolve as he learns the costs of unchecked ambition, or perhaps even assume a leadership role in the family if Conrad's power wanes. Another potential avenue is the development of the younger generation of characters, who may take center stage as they attempt to forge their own identities in the criminal world, potentially leading to internal family feuds or alliances with outside forces.

Speculation also abounds regarding the eventual fate of Conrad and Maeve Harrigan. With both characters having established themselves as central figures, the future of their relationship will be pivotal. Will Conrad remain the unchallenged patriarch, or will he face a challenge to his authority within the family? Given the show's focus on power struggles, it seems plausible that Maeve's own ambitions could lead to a more prominent role, particularly if she decides to pursue control of the family business herself.

Potential for Spin-offs or Prequels

Given the intricate world-building in MobLand and its focus on multiple intersecting characters, the show lends itself to potential spin-offs or even prequels. One of the most discussed spin-off ideas among fans is a deeper dive into the backstory of the Harrigan family. A prequel series could explore the rise of Conrad Harrigan, his early days in crime, and the steps he took to establish the family's empire. Such a show would provide valuable context for the current conflicts in MobLand, showing how the current generation of characters inherited a complex legacy.

The mythology of organized crime is rich with stories, and a prequel focusing on the criminal underworld before the events of MobLand would be a natural extension of the series. This could include the origins of key characters like Maeve and Conrad, offering a more nuanced view of their early relationships, the formative events that shaped their worldviews, and the methods they employed to build their criminal empire. Additionally, exploring the family's interactions with early rival gangs could set the stage for an even more dangerous world, laying the groundwork for the political and social networks that now control the criminal activities seen in the current series.

Another possible spin-off could focus on the world outside of the Harrigan family. Characters like Harry Da

Souza, who has long served as a fixer but is constantly on the edge of moral collapse, could have their own series focused on the business of handling messy situations for powerful people. A show focusing on Harry's work for other criminal organizations, or even branching out into other areas of corporate or political manipulation, could bring fresh perspectives to the established MobLand universe.

A further spin-off idea could explore the rise of the rival Stevenson family. Richard Stevenson and his children, who are introduced with less screen time but significant presence, have much room for growth. A prequel exploring their backstory, how they amassed their own criminal power, and their history with the Harrigans could offer another compelling layer to the world MobLand has built.

While the main series continues to explore the family dynamics at the heart of the show, these potential spin-offs would expand the MobLand universe, allowing for more stories to be told from different angles and perspectives. These ideas, though speculative, highlight the show's potential to build a lasting, interconnected universe that draws from its established world while introducing new narratives.

Interviews with the Creators About What Comes Next

In interviews, Guy Ritchie and the creative team behind MobLand have been relatively tight-lipped about specific details regarding future seasons, though they have offered some intriguing hints. Ritchie, known for his secretive approach to storytelling, has emphasized that MobLand will continue to evolve with its characters. "The show is about power and the consequences of living in a world where power is the currency," Ritchie said in a recent interview. "We want to dig deeper into that, exploring the moral cost of actions that seem small but snowball over time. There are some new dynamics coming—new characters, new stakes. I'm excited to push the boundaries."

Producer Jane Fitzgerald also touched on the challenges of continuing the series. "The complexity of the family dynamics will always remain at the forefront," she said, adding, "But there's room for growth. With each season, we plan to expand beyond the core family and look at the larger criminal ecosystem they interact with." Fitzgerald hinted that season two would begin to explore some of the unresolved tensions with outside criminal forces, specifically hinting at new alliances and betrayals that could push the Harrigans into unfamiliar territory.

When asked about possible spin-offs, Ritchie was cautious but open, acknowledging the "rich world" they had built. "There are stories within MobLand that deserve their own space," he explained. "We're in early discussions about expanding the world, but for now, the focus remains on the characters we've built and the story that's already in motion. We'll see where that takes us."

As the series progresses, both Ritchie and the production team seem committed to maintaining the show's focus on character development, even as they explore new avenues for the story. The future of MobLand, according to its creators, will balance staying true to the essence of the series while pushing its narrative into new and exciting directions.

Chapter 9: Behind-the-Scenes Stories and Anecdotes

Personal Stories from the Cast and Crew During Filming

Filming MobLand was as intricate and layered as the series itself. From the actors to the crew, everyone had stories to tell about their experiences on set, and many of these stories reveal the commitment and passion that went into creating the show.

Tom Hardy, who portrayed the conflicted fixer Harry Da Souza, was deeply invested in understanding the complexities of his character. In interviews, Hardy shared that he spent hours in preparation for certain scenes, especially the ones where Harry is required to suppress his emotions. "There was a lot of quiet work," he recalled, "just sitting with the character, thinking about how much Harry has internalized over the years. I wanted to make sure that his actions were always in tension with his thoughts. It was a very personal process."

Hardy also enjoyed moments of levity on set. The cast shared a strong camaraderie, and Hardy often recounted how, between takes, he and his co-stars would exchange jokes or even sing impromptu karaoke sessions during long shoots. "One day, we had a

16-hour shoot in a particularly grueling scene," Hardy laughed. "Pierce [Brosnan] started singing a classic tune, and by the end, we were all belting out 'Stand by Me.' It was a much-needed break after a long, emotionally taxing day. Those moments kept us grounded."

Pierce Brosnan, known for his stoic performances as Conrad Harrigan, offered a contrasting perspective on set. He was known for his methodical approach to the character, often researching the subtleties of organized crime families to add layers to his portrayal. However, Brosnan also found the filming process to be a bit more relaxed than his previous projects. "Guy [Ritchie] likes to keep things light between takes. There's always a sense of humor on set, even when we're working through some pretty intense material. It helps to stay grounded and keep the atmosphere creative."

Helen Mirren, who played Maeve Harrigan, had one of the most discussed transformations in the series. Known for her versatility, Mirren brought a sense of fierce intelligence to Maeve, making her one of the standout characters in the show. Behind the scenes, Mirren was equally invested, spending considerable time discussing the complexities of her role with Ritchie. "We spent a lot of time talking about Maeve's motivations," she said in a behind-the-scenes interview. "Her power is not just about being a boss. She's someone who knows the game, and she uses her knowledge and charm to manipulate those around her. There's always an edge to her, and that edge is what I wanted to bring to the role."

For Mirren, MobLand offered a unique challenge, especially since Maeve's character was so central to the story. "It's rare to see such a well-rounded female character in this genre," she continued. "That's what drew me to it. Maeve isn't just the wife or the matriarch; she's a strategist in her own right."

Fun Facts, Bloopers, and Interesting Tidbits

The filming of MobLand was not only challenging but also filled with moments of lightheartedness that the cast and crew took in stride. One notable fun fact comes from the early stages of production. The cast and crew were filming a particularly complex scene in an underground parking garage, where a pivotal confrontation between Harry and Conrad took place. As the cameras rolled, a stray dog wandered onto the set, completely unaware of the action unfolding around it. According to the crew, the dog sat next to the actors and calmly watched the scene unfold. Hardy and Brosnan both joked about the dog's "perfect timing," and it became a running joke among the cast that the dog was "the true star of the show."

On another occasion, while filming the tense standoff between the two crime families, an unexpected technical glitch occurred. The camera malfunctioned during a critical moment when Conrad is about to make a significant decision, causing the entire crew to halt production for several hours. While it caused frustration, the actors turned the downtime into an impromptu storytelling session, with Hardy entertaining the crew with stories from his past roles and Mirren discussing her career and acting techniques. This allowed the cast to bond during an otherwise stressful moment. The blooper from that incident—an unexpected cut to the camera crew laughing off-screen—made it into the show's promotional behind-the-scenes reel, much to everyone's amusement.

One of the most amusing moments, according to cast member anecdotes, occurred between Hardy and Brosnan. In a particularly intense scene involving the Harrigan family patriarch, Conrad, Hardy couldn't keep a straight face during one take. The scene was meant to be emotionally charged, but Hardy, being the consummate professional, kept breaking into fits of laughter after delivering his lines. "We were supposed to be having this dramatic exchange, but Tom couldn't stop laughing," Brosnan recalled with a grin. "I think it was because the setup felt so over-the-top, and Tom's energy was just contagious."

Unseen Challenges That the Team Faced During Production

While the set was full of camaraderie, the production of MobLand was not without its challenges. The most significant obstacle for the team was the complexity of shooting in various locations, especially when it came to coordinating the intense action sequences. These scenes, which often involved high-stakes confrontations between family members or criminal rivals, required precision and careful choreography. The logistics of coordinating multiple moving parts while ensuring that the actors could remain emotionally invested in the scene created tension on many days.

A particularly tricky sequence was the night shoot involving a large-scale shootout between rival factions. Not only did the actors need to be in top physical shape, but the crew had to carefully plan the sequence to account for the darkness, the timing of special effects, and the safety of the cast. According to one of the assistant directors, the shoot involved "countless rehearsals" and a team of experts who had to ensure that the gunfire and explosions were timed perfectly with the actors' performances. "There was no room for error," they explained. "The stakes were incredibly high, both in terms of physical safety and the emotional weight of the scene."

In addition to the physical demands of shooting these action-heavy sequences, the creative team had to constantly balance the show's quieter, character-driven moments with the larger-scale confrontations. There were instances where scenes that had been written with tension-heavy dialogue were challenging for actors to pull off convincingly, especially when filmed after long hours of more intense, action-driven scenes. Director

Guy Ritchie and the cinematography team worked closely to ensure a seamless transition between the emotionally charged and action-packed moments, with several late-night re-writes and adjustments made on the fly to refine certain dialogue-heavy scenes.

Another challenge the crew faced was the weather. London, where a large portion of the series was filmed, is known for its unpredictable weather, and filming outdoor scenes was often hindered by rain and strong winds. During one particular shoot, a critical scene involving Harry and Maeve at the family estate had to be rescheduled multiple times due to a sudden storm. As one of the producers put it, "The British weather always has the final say on this show. It took us longer than anticipated to get those pivotal shots, but we always made it work."

How the Show's Success Influenced Future Projects by the Same Team

The success of MobLand had a significant impact on the careers of the creative team and cast, many of whom were involved in subsequent projects following the show's debut. For Guy Ritchie, MobLand represented a shift in his career toward long-form television, allowing him to explore deeper, more complex narratives than the typically fast-paced style of his films. In interviews following the show's success, Ritchie discussed how the experience of working on MobLand gave him a new appreciation for the storytelling potential in episodic formats.

Ritchie's approach to character-driven narratives in MobLand was seen as a natural evolution of his filmmaking style. After the show's success, Ritchie was reportedly approached by multiple studios about developing new series within the same genre. His team, particularly producer Jane Fitzgerald, noted that the way MobLand was received by audiences helped to shift the perception of crime dramas on television. As Fitzgerald explained, "What MobLand proved was that there's room for more sophisticated crime dramas that are less about glorifying violence and more about the emotional and psychological complexity of its characters."

For the actors, MobLand was a transformative experience. The show gave Tom Hardy an opportunity to showcase his dramatic range in a way that had not been fully explored in his previous roles. The success of the series opened doors for him in both film and television, with multiple offers coming in after the show aired. Similarly, Helen Mirren's portrayal of Maeve Harrigan received widespread acclaim, and the role is often cited as one of the key performances of her career. As a result, Mirren's reputation as a powerhouse actress was further solidified, leading to additional roles in high-profile projects.

The show's success also led to increased interest in Guy Ritchie's collaborative partners, including producer

Fitzgerald and cinematographer John Mathieson, both of whom were involved in subsequent high-profile productions. The chemistry between Ritchie and his crew on MobLand led to plans for future collaborations, including potential spinoffs, which have been discussed in early development meetings.

Ultimately, the success of MobLand provided the creative team with a platform to experiment with new ideas, exploring further character development and expanding the show's world. The impact of the show on both its cast and creators is undeniable, as it opened new doors for everyone involved while also setting the stage for future crime dramas and spin-offs that will undoubtedly draw inspiration from the formula that made MobLand a success.

Conclusion

Recap of the Key Points Covered in the Book

MobLand has firmly established itself as a pivotal entry in the crime drama genre, blending gritty storytelling with intricate character development and a visually distinct style. This book has explored the many facets of the series, from the early concept and development phases to its impact on both the industry and its viewers. The unique vision behind MobLand, spearheaded by Guy Ritchie, was explored, focusing on how the show's structure deviates from traditional crime dramas by delving deep into the moral conflicts and psychological landscapes of its characters.

Throughout this book, we've examined the central figures in the story, such as Harry Da Souza, Conrad Harrigan, and Maeve Harrigan, and how their performances, particularly by Tom Hardy, Pierce Brosnan, and Helen Mirren, elevated the narrative. The interactions between these characters, the shifting allegiances, and the family dynamics form the backbone of MobLand's plot. By digging into the cast's personal experiences and behind-the-scenes stories, we've seen how their work contributed to bringing the complex world of MobLand to life.

The production and filmmaking process behind MobLand was detailed, highlighting the challenges the crew faced—from location choices and set design to the technical aspects of filming action sequences. The creative decisions made in terms of cinematography, sound design, and music were critical to setting the tone of the series, contributing to the immersive and atmospheric world Ritchie crafted.

The critical reception and audience feedback were also explored, showing how MobLand struck a balance between critical acclaim and fan enthusiasm. Despite some mixed reviews, the series has gained a strong following, solidifying its place in the cultural conversation surrounding modern crime dramas. The success of MobLand has opened up possibilities for future seasons, spin-offs, and new directions, ensuring its relevance in an ever-evolving entertainment landscape.

Finally, the cultural impact of MobLand was discussed, from its influence on the crime drama genre to the way it resonates with global audiences. The show has sparked conversations on societal perceptions of crime, family, and loyalty, adding to its lasting significance. Its ability to engage fans and spark a dedicated fan culture has made it an enduring force in the television landscape.

Reflection on the Lasting Impact of "MobLand" within the Crime Drama Genre

MobLand's influence within the crime drama genre is already being felt. While the genre has long been known for its focus on anti-heroes, MobLand manages to stand out by honing in on the moral complexities of its characters. The show does not glorify crime but instead invites viewers to understand the multifaceted nature of criminal life and the emotional toll it takes on those involved. In a landscape flooded with traditional mobster narratives, MobLand's approach—focusing on familial struggles, psychological tension, and shifting power dynamics—offers something new.

The show represents a subtle evolution of the genre, where character exploration takes precedence over action-driven plots. This shift allows for more nuanced storytelling, where viewers are drawn into the psychological battles within families rather than simply following the external conflict. By placing so much focus on family loyalty and the impact of legacy, MobLand challenges traditional crime drama tropes, offering a refreshing perspective that is both familiar and innovative.

Moreover, MobLand plays into the ongoing trend of crime dramas that explore the darker sides of human nature. Shows like Breaking Bad and The Sopranos paved the way for anti-hero-centered stories that delve into the psyche of those who commit crimes. MobLand follows in their footsteps but further emphasizes the complexity of these characters through its focus on emotional depth. The show's focus on the mental and emotional strains of its characters—particularly Harry Da Souza's internal conflict—elevates the genre, giving it a more introspective and philosophical dimension.

The show's approach to its characters, pacing, and moral dilemmas signals a shift in how crime dramas will be approached in the future. Rather than merely showing crimes and their consequences, MobLand challenges viewers to question the motivations behind these actions, exploring the fine line between right and wrong. As more series follow in its footsteps, we may see a further evolution of the genre where the focus is not just on the criminal underworld, but on the people caught in its web, their moral struggles, and their personal journeys.

Final Thoughts on the Legacy and Continued Relevance of the Series

Looking ahead, MobLand has the potential to continue its relevance in the evolving landscape of television. Its legacy is rooted not only in its strong performances and intricate storytelling but also in its willingness to break from traditional crime drama formulas. The series is part of a new wave of television where character-driven stories are becoming central to the genre, moving away from the glorification of crime to a more nuanced exploration of human nature.

As MobLand grows, it is clear that its strength lies in its ability to keep audiences engaged with characters that are morally ambiguous, relatable, and unpredictable. The family at the center of the story is not a typical mafia family, but rather a complex web of relationships that evolve and fracture in ways that feel fresh within the genre. The show's focus on emotional stakes rather than merely external threats makes it stand out from other offerings in the crime drama world.

The series also has the unique ability to influence future crime dramas and expand its own universe. The possibility of spin-offs and prequels, as well as the exploration of new characters and conflicts, means that the world of MobLand could grow far beyond what was originally imagined. There is potential to dive deeper into the histories of supporting characters or explore new factions that will interact with the core families in exciting and unexpected ways.

As its influence continues to ripple through the television landscape, MobLand will undoubtedly serve as a reference point for creators looking to explore the intersection of crime, power, and familial bonds. The series has proven that there is a thirst for crime dramas that not only entertain but also provoke thought, challenge conventions, and create characters who linger long after the screen fades to black.

The cultural footprint of MobLand will continue to expand, particularly as it resonates with audiences who are craving deeper stories. As the genre progresses, MobLand stands as a powerful example of how crime dramas can evolve into thoughtful, character-driven narratives that engage audiences not just with action, but with introspection and emotional depth.

In conclusion, MobLand will be remembered not just for its compelling storylines or gripping performances, but for its ability to shift perceptions about what crime dramas can achieve. Its legacy is still being written, and its impact will likely be felt for years to come, both within the genre and in the broader landscape of television storytelling. The show's blend of emotional complexity, power struggles, and morally conflicted characters marks it as a key chapter in the modern evolution of the crime drama genre.

Printed in Dunstable, United Kingdom